This book belongs to

....

....

This edition printed in 2015 by Alligator publishing Ltd.
Cupcake is an imprint of Alligator Publishing Ltd.
2nd Floor, 314 Regents Park Road, London, N3 2JX

Written by Katherine Sully
Illustrated by Rebecca Elliot

Printed in China 0157

Penguins Can't Fly

cupcake

Once there were two little penguin chicks. Their eggs had hatched on the same day and they knew each other's names – Quentin and Billy.

When they were baby chicks they played together.
They played peep-po!, they called each other silly
names: Tintin! Chilly Billy!

As the young chicks grew up, their games changed.
Billy like playing Hide and Seek...

...but it was a bit rough for Quentin.

Quentin like building with ice bricks – but it was too dull for Billy. Though they did make a den together once.

You see the two little penguins were quite different.

Quentin liked knowing things, like what all the fish were called,

how many different types of snow there were…

…and, best of all, how far away the stars were.

Billy loved doing
things, like skating
down steep slopes,

hurling snowballs...

...and doing
bellyflops
along the ice.

In fact, Billy was always getting told off.

Especially at school. You see, Billy just couldn't sit still. He tried to be good but he always ended up being told off.

"Sit still, Billy," his teacher was forever saying. "How are you ever going to look after an egg when you're older if you can't learn to sit still."

$1 \times 1 =$
$2 \times 3 =$

One particular morning, Billy fidgeted so much that the teacher told him off…again.

At lunchtime, Quentin couldn't find Billy so he ate his lunch alone. He was gazing at the clouds when some gulls flew past.

"Hello," squawked one gull. "What are you looking at?"

"I'm looking at the clouds," replied Quentin. "I think we're in for a snowstorm."

"A snow storm?" squawked the gull.

"Yes," said Quentin. "It's not good weather for birds."

"How would you know?" said the other gull. "You're not a proper bird!"

"I am a proper bird!" said Quentin. "I have feathers and a beak, and I hatched from an egg."

"Ah," squawked the gull. "But you can't fly, can you?"

Before Quentin could think of a reply, the gull had swooped down and stolen his lunch.

That night, Quentin couldn't sleep. He went to sit on his favourite rock and gazed up at the sky. Through a tiny gap in the clouds he could see some stars twinkling.

"I'll never be able to reach you," he told the stars quietly, "because I'm a bird that can't fly."

Then he heard the sound of a pebble being thrown into the water.

"Who's there?" asked Quentin.

"It's me, Billy," Billy replied.

"Oh, couldn't you sleep either?" asked Quentin.

"I'm going away," said Billy. "I'm fed up with being told off."

"I wouldn't do that, if I were you," said Quentin. "I think we're in for a snowstorm."

But there was no reply. Billy had gone.

Quentin was right. The next day there was the most terrific snowstorm. You could barely see your flipper in front of your eyes. Everyone huddled together for warmth. All day the wind howled and the snow fell.

That evening, Quentin heard a voice calling:
"Billy! Billy!" It was Billy's mum. "Have you seen
Billy?" No one could think where he could be.
Except for Quentin.

Quentin set off right away. It was dark but
Quentin found his way by looking at the stars.
At last, he came to the den that he and Billy had
built when they were chicks.

"Billy, are you there?" asked Quentin?
"Yes," shivered Billy.
"Your mum's worried about you."" said Quentin.
"Is she?" asked Billy. "OK, I'll come home."

The two friends walked home together.

"You were right about the snowstorm," said Billy. And Quentin told Billy about the gulls.

"Of course we're proper birds," said Billy. "We just swim instead of flying."

"I'm not sure I'll be able to swim," said Quentin.

"Wait until we start swimming lessons!" said Billy. "It's going to be great!"

And Quentin didn't have to wait very long. That week at school they practiced lining up, hopping, skimming and twisting – on the ice.

Billy had a great time and didn't get into trouble once. In fact, the teacher said: "Well done, Billy!" several times!

So when it was time to take their first dive, Quentin wasn't looking forward to it.

"Don't worry," said Billy, "It's going to be great!" Billy leapt into the water making a huge splash. Quentin stood at the edge of the rock and gazed into the water.

Just then, Billy shot back out of the water.

"Wow! Tintin," he said, "You're going to love the amazing fish down here!"

"Oh but I don't think I can…" started Quentin.

Just then, Billy shot back out of the water onto the ice.

"Wow! Tintin," he said, "You won't believe the amazing fish and weird stuff there is down there."

"Really?" asked Quentin.

"Yes, I don't know any of the names," said Billy, "but you will."

"Oh but I don't think I can…" started Quentin. But it was too late. Billy took hold of his flipper and together…

…they splashed into the sea…

...and Quentin flew...

...under the water.

And Billy was right – what
an amazing sight!

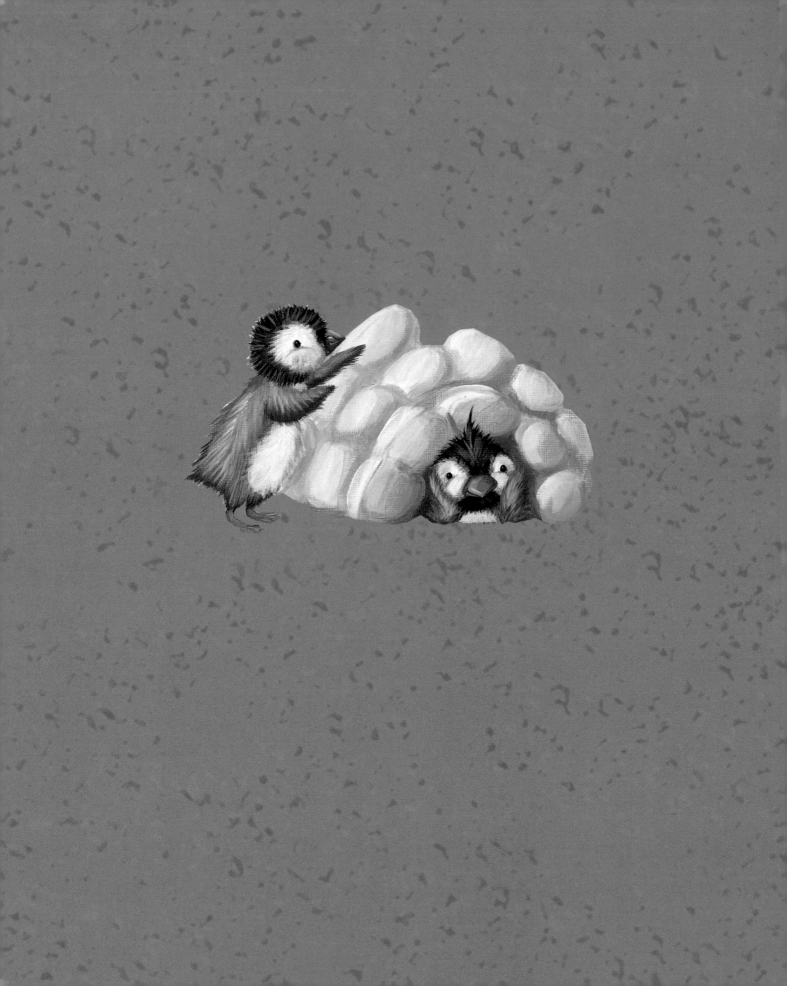